Jackrabbit

by Jonathan London
illustrated by Deborah Kogan Ray

Crown Publishers, Inc., New York

For Kelly and Emily and Faline—
whose story this is;
with warm thanks to Marjorie Davis,
wildlife rehabilitator — J. L.

Another for Raymond,
my best friend — D.K.R.

Published by Crown Publishers, Inc.,
a Random House company, 201 East 50th Street,
New York, New York 10022

CROWN is a trademark of Crown Publishers, Inc.
Reprinted by arrangement with Crown Publishers, Inc.,
a Random House company.
Printed in the U.S.A.
Library of Congress Cataloging-in-Publication Data
London, Jonathan
Jackrabbit / by Jonathan London ; illustrated by Deborah
Kogan Ray. — 1st ed.
p. cm.
Summary: When a baby jackrabbit's home is destroyed
by developers, she is cared for by a human family until
she is big enough to live on her own in the wild.
[1. Rabbits—Fiction. 2. Wildlife rescue—Fiction.]
I. Ray, Deborah Kogan, ill. II. Title. III. Title:
Jackrabbit.
PZ7.L8432Jac 1996
[E]—dc20   94-1080

ISBN 0-517-59657-1 (trade)
      0-517-59658-X (lib. bdg.)

10 9 8 7 6 5 4 3 2

First Edition

Five jackrabbits curl snug
and warm in their nest.

Suddenly, the earth trembles.
The ground roars.
Mother Jackrabbit
drums her hind foot in warning
and noses her litter out.

The hares flee through the orchard.
Jackrabbit, the runt, can't keep up.

The bulldozers are coming.
Jackrabbit can hear the trees
crashing behind her.
She dives down a hole.

Later, when everything grows quiet,
Jackrabbit drags herself out.
It's dark. The trees
are crushed to the ground.

There's something behind her—
yellow eyes in the dark.
Jackrabbit dashes away
as quick as her little legs
will carry her.

A dog barks. A light flashes.
Jackrabbit freezes.
"Scat!" hollers a woman.
The cat scats.
"Shush!" she hushes the dog,
and chases after Jackrabbit.

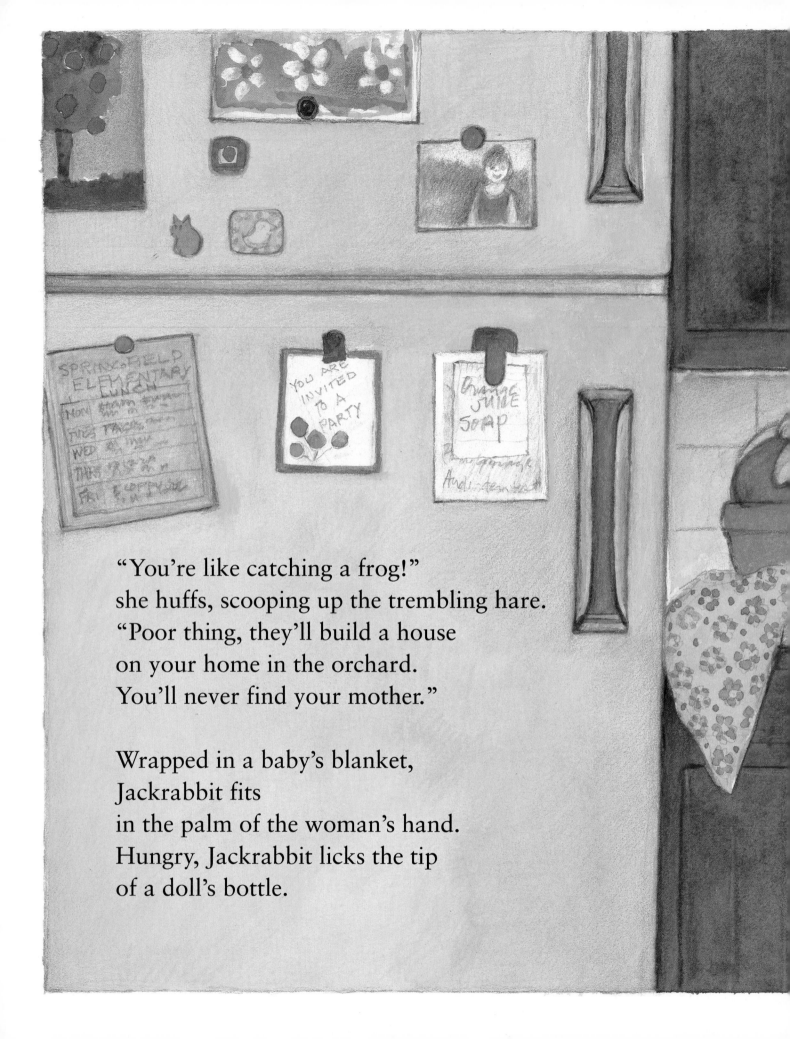

"You're like catching a frog!"
she huffs, scooping up the trembling hare.
"Poor thing, they'll build a house
on your home in the orchard.
You'll never find your mother."

Wrapped in a baby's blanket,
Jackrabbit fits
in the palm of the woman's hand.
Hungry, Jackrabbit licks the tip
of a doll's bottle.

"Good night, Jackie," the woman says,
tucking Jackrabbit in.
Jackie curls by the stove,
the milk warm in her belly.
And soon she is asleep.

Two hours later, she wakes,
grunting with hunger.
"Ooh, just like a baby," coos the woman
as she warms another bottle.

Every night for weeks,
it is the same.
Sometimes a girl feeds her.
Sometimes a man.

But the day comes
when Jackie can eat peaches,
wild clover and alfalfa,
blackberries and apples and bananas—
bananas are her favorite.

Whenever the woman
lets her out of her cage,
Jackie races around the room—
so excited, she leaps
and turns in mid-air
and lands running
in the opposite direction.

When the woman calls her name,
Jackie hops back,
snuggles beside her,
and licks the woman's fingers
with her rough pink tongue.

Over the weeks,
Jackie grows by leaps and bounds.
Little by little,
the woman stops handling her.

Then one day, the woman grabs her,
clutches her tight.
Jackie gives her a rabbit punch—
half in fun, half in fright.

The woman strokes her long ears,
then sets her gently in the grass.
"There are still lots of fields and trees
around here, Jackie," she says.
Her voice trembles.
She gives Jackie a nudge.

Jackie just sits there
twitching her whiskers.
Then she takes a few hops.
Stops. And hops back to the woman.

"Go!" the woman commands,
and tears shine in her eyes.
Jackie sniffs the breeze—
no bananas grow here,
but warm blackberries
dangle in the sun—

and then she dashes away.

Every few weeks,
Jackie returns.
Looks at the house.
Looks for the woman.
Then turns back to the fields.

One day, she's nibbling
in a blueberry patch
with a big jack
when they hear a sound.

Jackie's mate
grinds his teeth,
drums his hind foot,
and plunges through the wild grass.
Jackie leaps right behind him.

"J-A-C-K-I-E!" cries a voice.
Jackie spins in her tracks
and stops.
The woman holds her hand
over her heart. Jackie's heart
thumpthumpthumps—
as fast as her mate racing away.

Jackie rises and sniffs the air.
She stands for an endless minute—
twitching her nose, twisting her ears—

then turns away
and bounds after her mate.
She's flowing with the grasses,
running with the wind,
racing cloud shadows and leaping
like a jackrabbit—
like the jackrabbit she is.

Weeks later, she curls
with her babies in a nest
woven with fur pulled
from her own body.

Sometimes she dreams
about her bed of straw by the stove.
About romping around and spinning
in mid-air.
About licking the woman's fingers
for the salt taste there.

And sometimes she dreams about bananas.